The Little Engine That Could™
AND THE FIRE RESCUE

written by Megan E. Bryant
based on the original story by Watty Piper
illustrated by Loretta Lustig

Platt & Munk, Publishers • New York

For brave firefighters everywhere.—M.E.B.
For Frank, who almost set the barn on fire.—L.L.

Copyright © 2003 by Platt & Munk, Publishers. All rights reserved. Published by Platt & Munk, Publishers. a division of Grosset & Dunlap, which is a division of Penguin Young Readers Group, 345 Hudson Street, New York, NY 10014. THE LITTLE ENGINE THAT COULD, engine design, and "I THINK I CAN," PLATT & MUNK, and GROSSET & DUNLAP are trademarks of Penguin Group (USA) Inc. Registered in U.S. Patent and Trademark Office. Published simultaneously in Canada. Printed in the U.S.A.

Library of Congress Cataloging-in-Publication Data is available.

ISBN 0-448-43279-X   A B C D E F G H I J

One Saturday morning, the Little Engine That Could set out to visit her good friend Fire Truck Fred at the Piney Vale Fire Department.

"Hi, Little Blue!" Fire Truck Fred called.

"Hi, Fred!" replied the Little Blue Engine.

Two black-and-white Dalmatian dogs ran out of the station. They barked happily when they saw the Little Blue Engine. She laughed. "And hello to you, too, Jack and Sally," she said to the fire dogs.

Just then, Chief Dan came out of the fire station. "Hi there, Little Blue! Ready for your tour?"

The Little Blue Engine nodded happily. Chief Dan was going to tell her all about the firehouse!

"Well, on the first floor there's an office, a classroom, and a garage," Chief Dan began.

"The garage is my room," Fire Truck Fred added. "That's where I get washed and get checkups from the mechanic. That's also where I rest when there isn't a fire to put out."

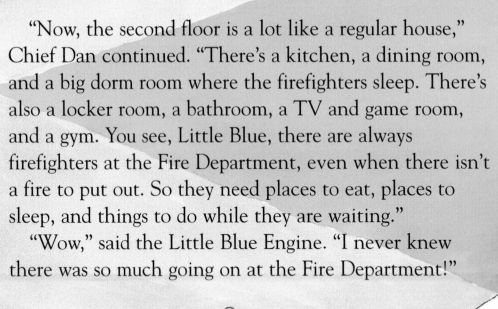

"Now, the second floor is a lot like a regular house," Chief Dan continued. "There's a kitchen, a dining room, and a big dorm room where the firefighters sleep. There's also a locker room, a bathroom, a TV and game room, and a gym. You see, Little Blue, there are always firefighters at the Fire Department, even when there isn't a fire to put out. So they need places to eat, places to sleep, and things to do while they are waiting."

"Wow," said the Little Blue Engine. "I never knew there was so much going on at the Fire Department!"

Suddenly, a loud alarm pierced the air.

"Chief Dan!" yelled a firefighter. "There's a two-alarm blaze—the Twin Oaks Train Station!"

"The Twin Oaks Train Station!" the Little Blue Engine exclaimed. "My friend Rosie the Red Engine lives there!"

"Don't worry, Little Blue," said Fire Truck Fred. "We're going to do everything we can to keep everyone safe."

Several firefighters rushed out of the station wearing large boots, heavy gear, and protective helmets. They quickly boarded Fire Truck Fred, along with Jack and Sally. Fire Truck Fred raced down the street, his siren wailing and lights flashing.

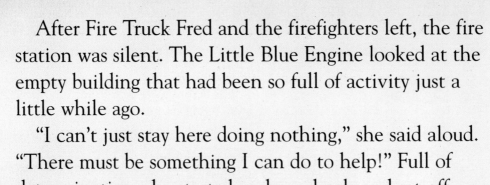

After Fire Truck Fred and the firefighters left, the fire station was silent. The Little Blue Engine looked at the empty building that had been so full of activity just a little while ago.

"I can't just stay here doing nothing," she said aloud. "There must be something I can do to help!" Full of determination, she started up her wheels and set off down the tracks to the Twin Oaks Train Station.

Soon the Little Engine arrived at the train station. Thick, black clouds of smoke billowed into the sky. She spotted Fire Truck Fred.

"Fire Truck Fred!" she called out loudly. "What can I do to help?"

"Just stay back, Little Blue," Fire Truck Fred yelled back. "Fire fighting is very dangerous! Everything is under control. Everyone's out of the station. All we have to do now is put out the fire."

"Okay," the Little Blue Engine replied, relieved that everyone was safe. She saw Rosie the Red Engine.

"Rosie, I'm so glad you're okay!" she called to her friend.

The Little Blue Engine backed down the tracks, stopping in front of a storage shed not far from the train station.

There, she could see the firefighters spraying powerful blasts of water at the fire.

Anna Ambulance and Dr. Beth had also arrived to make sure that all the people who had been inside the station were fine.

Everyone had a job to do. Everyone was helping out. Everyone except the Little Blue Engine.

Just then the Little Blue Engine heard loud barking. She looked around. It was Jack and Sally! The two dogs stood in front of the little shed. They barked again and began to whimper.

"What's wrong, Sally? What is it, Jack?" the Little
Engine That Could asked. And then she saw: Smoke
was coming from the shed! The Little Blue Engine
could hear a faint whimpering sound. Someone
was trapped inside!

A furry brown face appeared in the window—it was a dog! "Oh no!" the Little Blue Engine exclaimed. Now she knew why Jack and Sally were barking: They were trying to attract help for the poor dog trapped in the shed! But with all the commotion at the train station, no one had noticed them.

"I can't get off the track to rescue the dog myself," the Little Blue Engine said, "but I think I *can* do something to bring help right away." The Little Engine That Could took a deep breath and blew her whistle as hard as she could.

Wheeeeeeeeeeeet!
Wheeeeeeeeeeeet!
Wheeeeeeeeeeeet!

Fire Truck Fred and Chief Dan looked up at the sound of the Little Blue Engine's whistle.

"There's a dog trapped in the shed!" the Little Blue Engine yelled. "Somebody, help!"

The fire in the train station was almost completely out, so Chief Dan nodded at two of his firefighters. "John, Mary, let's go rescue that dog!"

The two firefighters ran to the shed. They used their axes to chop through the door. Then, being careful to stay low to the ground, they crawled inside.

The Little Blue Engine held her breath as she waited for the firefighters to come out. After a few moments, Firefighter John appeared, carrying the dog. The crowd cheered!

But where was Firefighter Mary?

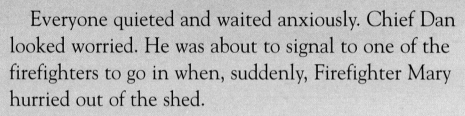

Everyone quieted and waited anxiously. Chief Dan looked worried. He was about to signal to one of the firefighters to go in when, suddenly, Firefighter Mary hurried out of the shed.

In her arms were three plump, squirming puppies!

She set them on the ground a safe distance from the shed. The crowd clapped and cheered again as the mama dog rushed over to her puppies and nuzzled them gently.

Fire Truck Fred drove over to the Little Blue Engine. "Great job, Little Blue!" he said with a big smile. "You saved that dog and her puppies!"

"*I* didn't save them," said the Little Engine That Could. "Jack and Sally were the ones who found the dogs and barked until someone noticed them. And those brave firefighters were the ones who rescued the dogs and brought them to safety. I wish I could have been a bigger help, but all *I* did was blow my whistle."

Chief Dan walked over. "Little Blue, fighting a fire and rescuing people takes teamwork and cooperation—no one can do it alone," he explained. "You, Jack, Sally, and the firefighters all worked together to save those dogs. You're *all* heroes!"

"Really?" the Little Blue Engine said.

"Absolutely," said Chief Dan. "But we still have one problem: What are we going to do with this nice dog and her pups? They need a good home."

"Oh, I know!" said the Little Blue Engine. "I can take them to Dr. Judy, the animal doctor in Piney Vale. She always knows nice people who want to adopt dogs—and pups!"

"Great idea, Little Blue!" said Fire Truck Fred.

Chief Dan carefully settled the mama dog and her puppies into the Little Blue Engine's cab before climbing aboard Fire Truck Fred. "Thanks for your help, Little Blue!" Chief Dan called as they drove off. Fire Truck Fred beeped his horn.

The Little Blue Engine grinned proudly as she rolled down the track on her way to Dr. Judy. Now she knew that she really had helped today—by working together with her friends!

Here are some fire safety tips from the Little Engine That Could™:

1 Make sure your house has smoke detectors with working batteries, and at least one fire extinguisher. A good idea is to change the batteries in your smoke detectors every fall and spring.

2 Never, ever play with matches, lighters, candles, or fire!

3 If your clothes catch on fire, STOP, DROP, AND ROLL! STOP—don't run around. DROP—to the ground and cover your face with your hands. ROLL—back and forth until the flames are out.

4 If there is smoke, stay close to the ground. Smoke rises up to the ceiling, so it will be easier to breathe near the floor.

5 If there is a fire, don't open any closed doors without touching them first. If the door feels COOL, open it slowly. If it is WARM or HOT, don't open it at all!

6 Don't hide from firefighters. They might seem scary since they will look very big in their suits and will make funny breathing noises, but they are your friends and will help you get to safety.

7 Have a fire drill with your family so everyone knows what to do in case of a fire.